LEGENDS

iHERO

BEOWULF

STEVE BARLOW + STEVE SKIDMORE
ART BY ANDREW TUNNEY

EDGE
FRANKLIN WATTS

Franklin Watts
First published in Great Britain in 2017
by The Watts Publishing Group

Text © Steve Barlow and Steve Skidmore 2017
Illustrations © Andrew Tunney 2017
Cover design: Peter Scoulding
Executive Editor: Adrian Cole

ISBN 978 1 4451 5225 7
ebook ISBN 978 1 4451 5226 4
Library ebook ISBN 978 1 4451 5227 1

1 3 5 7 9 10 8 6 4 2

Printed in Great Britain

MIX
Paper from
responsible sources
FSC® C104740

Franklin Watts
An imprint of
Hachette Children's Group
Part of The Watts Publishing Group
Carmelite House
50 Victoria Embankment
London EC4Y 0DZ

An Hachette UK Company
www.hachette.co.uk

www.franklinwatts.co.uk

How to be a Legend

Throughout the ages, great men and women have performed deeds so mighty that their names have passed into legend.

Could YOU be one of them?

In this book, you are Beowulf, the hero of the adventure. You must make decisions that will affect how the adventure unfolds.

Each section of this book is numbered. At the end of most sections, you will have to make a choice. The choice you make will take you to a different section of the book.

Some of your choices will help you to complete the adventure successfully. But choose carefully, some of your decisions could be fatal!

If you fail, then start the adventure again, and learn from your mistake.

If you choose wisely, you will succeed!

Are you ready to be a hero? Have you got what it takes to become a legend?

You are Beowulf, heroic warrior of the Geats, a bold and warlike Scandinavian people.

You have already helped your neighbour, the King of Denmark, by destroying Grendel. This monster had killed many of the king's most loyal men, but you fought and defeated it with your bare hands.

You hoped the threat was over, but the very next night, Grendel's mother appeared and killed even more men.

You tracked the monster to its lair beneath a lake and, following a ferocious battle, cut off her head.

Since those dark but triumphant days, you have become king of your people. But now a new threat has emerged — a threat that will take all your skill and courage to overcome.

Go to section 1.

Your warriors are gathered in the great Feast Hall of your people. They are celebrating the success of their latest hunt around a roaring fire, eating, drinking, and cheering your blind harpist Osric as he sings of their brave deeds. The songs of the harpist are not just entertainment — they hold all the memory and wisdom of your people.

At the height of the festivities, the great doors of the hall open with a crash. Snow blows in on the cold wind. Silence falls as a messenger enters.

"Lord King," he croaks, "I bring terrible news. Many villages in the north of your lands have been destroyed and their inhabitants have been killed!"

You are angry. Who dares disturb the peace of your realm? You call your warriors to arms. "We ride at once!"

Osric steps forward. "My lord, hear my advice."

If you wish to listen to Osric's advice, go to 18.

If you wish to set off at once, go to 34.

2

"We will rest here first," you say.

Agnar disagrees. "There's no shelter here! And who knows what this Magnus may do as we rest?"

You will not listen. "The men are tired."

Wrapped in your cloak, you try to sleep, but soon realise Agnar is right. There is no shelter in these ruins from the snow, the wind and the cold.

You hear a footstep behind you and look up to see a dark, cloaked figure holding a staff. The stranger speaks. "I am Magnus."

Go to 41.

3

You tear down the huts and build a funeral pyre to send the spirits of your dead comrades to Valhalla, the hall of fallen heroes.

As you forage for more wood, you feel a presence behind you. You turn, reaching for your sword. Standing there is a tall, cloaked figure holding a staff. The stranger speaks. "I am Magnus. You have defeated my blood-brides, but you will not prevail against me."

Go to 41.

4

You lead your men into the graveyard. As you reach its centre, you come across a dip in the ground. It holds two mounds; one glints with steel, the other shines with the gleam of gold.

"A treasure hoard," you say, "and a stockpile of weapons!" Some of your men reach for the gold. Some of them reach for a weapon.

If you want to order your men to take only the weapons, go to 21.

If you would like to tell them to help themselves to anything, go to 43.

5

You strike at the ghosts with your sword, but hit nothing. Too late, you realise that fighting a ghost is like fighting smoke!

Magnus points his staff at you. You cannot move; you drop your sword. All your efforts to break free are in vain.

The enchanter gives a harsh laugh. "Fool! You are in my power!"

A burst of terrible light flares from the staff. As it surrounds you, your life force drains from your body.

You've allowed yourself to be spooked by ghosts! Go to 1.

6

You thrust your sword towards the blood-bride. Your blade goes right through the woman's body, but it has no effect! Too late you remember that blood-brides are undead; a wound that would kill a living person will not harm them.

Before you can make any further move, the blood-bride is upon you. Her claws slice at your throat. You feel the darkness of death descend upon you.

Heroes of legend are not beaten by bloodsuckers! Go to 1.

7

"Make my ship ready," you order.

You and your crew set sail. Soon you are battling your way through ice floes and rough, foaming seas.

Then, the water all around your ship seems to boil. A monstrous, eel-like creature with a dragon's head bursts up through the waves, rising high above your ship. Then it plunges down to take your vessel in its thick coils.

Your men fight bravely, but weapons are useless against the monster.

Agnar appears at your side. "This is a creature of the gods, and only they can fight it! Call upon the gods of our people — Thor or Loki — to help us!"

If you want to call upon Thor, go to 29.
If you want to call upon Loki, go to 40.

8

You lead your men to the village square. From between the huts, beautiful women appear. Their hair is wild, their faces pale; they are crying and clearly terrified.

"Our men are sick!" they wail. "There is no one to protect us from the enchanter Magnus! Please, you must help us!"

If you wish to send your followers to help the sick men, go to 15.

If you wish to question the women more closely, go to 35.

9

You drop your weapons and throw off your mail shirt before swimming for the bank. The men who follow your example come ashore nearby. Those who refuse to give up their weapons are swept over the falls with despairing cries.

You are tired, chilled to the bone and defenceless. But as you follow a track leading away from the river, you see in the distance a ruined castle bathed in an eerie glow.

Lightning flickers between its broken turrets.

You stare at the castle. "I think we have found the lair of Magnus."

Go to 26.

10

You descend the stairs. Soon, even the faint light of the stars disappears. Bats fly at you with whirring wings, their sharp claws catching at your hair, face and hands. You lash at them with your sword, but to no effect.

While the bats distract you, you feel strong, clammy fingers grasp your body. A flaming torch splutters into life and, to your horror, you realise you are surrounded by flesh-eating ghouls. You groan — what else would you expect to find in an enchanter's crypt?

The foul creatures moan and slobber in anticipation, then, mouths wide and teeth clacking, they attack! The crypt echoes to your screams.

You have been careless — you can't beat ghoul power! Go to 1.

11

The track leads down into the Dark Fens and quickly disappears. Soon you are wading thigh-deep in dark water and stinking, clinging mud. Lights appear in the distance, and some of your men head for them.

"A village!" they cry. "We will find shelter there."

"Ignore the lights!" you call. "They are will-o'-the-wisps! They will lead you astray!"

But your men ignore the warning. You hear terrified shrieks and howls as they sink into the mire.

To head for the graveyard, go to 4.
If you want to press on through the marshes, go to 32.

12

"Thor!" you cry. "Come to our aid!"

The clouds part and Thor appears. But when the thunder god sees your enemy, he scowls and shakes his head. "Fenrir is the son of my brother, Loki. If I take your side against him, Loki will be angry."

Thor vanishes into the clouds. You open your mouth to call on Loki for help, but it is too late. Fenrir has killed all of your men, and now he is coming for you, jaws wide open. One snap, and your quest is over.

Your adventure has ended almost before it began. Go to 1.

13

"Who are you, child?" you demand. "How did you come here?"

"You must help me, quickly," she cries. "The enchanter may come back ..."

But you remember the village shaman's warning. Magnus is a shape-changer!

To see the girl's reflection, go to 42.
If you wish to accuse the girl of being Magnus, go to 47.

The first village you come to is a fire-blackened ruin. As your men search for survivors, a strange figure looms out of the snow and mist.

You realise this must be the shaman, the wise

man of the village who has somehow escaped the destruction of his home.

"Who has done this?" you ask.

"A dark enchanter," he replies. "His name is Magnus. He has powerful magic and can change his shape at will. Only by looking at his reflection can you see him as he really is."

"We must find this Magnus," you say, "and destroy him!"

If you decide to rest before going in search of Magnus, go to 2.

If you would rather press on at once, go to 30.

15

"Look in the huts," you order.

Your men spread out and disappear into dark hut doorways. There is a moment's silence. Then terrible screams ring out from every hut. Your men are crying out in mortal dread. You draw your sword to help them. Hearing a step behind you, you turn to see a dark, cloaked figure holding a staff. The stranger speaks. "I am Magnus."

Go to 41.

"Magnus has done enough damage here," you say. "Let us save what we can."

The moment your men start to pick up the kittens, they transform into gigantic demon cats with glowing red eyes. They spit at the men trying

to rescue them. Those they have attacked fall, screaming, and die. You recognise the terrible creatures from your harpist's songs. "Palug cats! More devilry of Magnus — the foul creatures spit venom!" Your warning comes too late — half your men are already dead.

To order your men to run, go to 44.
To order them to stay and fight, go to 22.

17

You begin your climb. The rock crumbles between your fingers and you have to test every hand- and toe-hold carefully.

You are nearing the top of the wall when flocks of ravens and gore-crows rise from the towers of the castle. More creatures of Magnus!

Cawing madly, the birds attack you. You cannot spare a hand to draw your sword as they peck at your face, your hair, your fingers. You cannot hold on. You fall, screaming, down towards the jagged rocks of the ravine. Death swiftly claims you.

Legends don't let themselves be henpecked by angry birds! Go to 1.

You take Osric by the arm. "What do you foresee?"

Osric's sightless eyes seem to look into the future. "My lord, your enemy is powerful. I sense that he has raised the powers of the Earth against you. If you travel to the northlands by sea, you will meet with the Midgard Serpent. You must call upon Thor the Thunderer for aid. But if you go by land, you will encounter the

wolf Fenrir. Then you must call upon Loki the Trickster, he is Fenrir's father and the only one the wolf will obey."

Go to 34.

19

"Yes," you say, "we are all weary." You follow the woman into a hut.

On the bed inside lies a warrior of your people. He is dead. His throat has been cut. Both his tunic and the walls of the hut are caked in blood.

You turn to see the woman reaching for you, with fingernails that have changed into razor-sharp claws. Her mouth gapes to reveal sharp pointed teeth. You realise too late that the woman is a blood-bride — an evil, undead creature that survives by drinking human blood!

You brace yourself to meet her attack. But the woman hisses and recoils from you as a tall, cloaked figure holding a staff appears behind her. Snarling in disappointed rage, she leaves the hut. The stranger speaks. "I am Magnus."

Go to 41.

20

"We can't escape the falls with our armour and weapons," gasps Agnar.

You refuse to listen. "We will have more enemies to fight! I will not surrender my arms!"

You try to swim for the bank, but your armour weighs you down and the current is too strong. You are swept towards the falls and carried over. You are smashed against the rocks below the falls. Life ebbs from your broken body.

Armour and weapons are of no use to a dead hero! Go to 1.

21

"Take only weapons," you order. "Do not touch the treasure."

Your men take weapons from the pile. As they do so, the earth shudders and bursts open. From every grave, figures in armour rise up, their skin hanging in tatters on their bones. They are dreygur, the most feared creatures of the undead realm — immensely strong flesh-eating zombies of slain warriors.

But your men are armed. With sword, spear

and bow in hand, they are brave enough to face
even these terrible foes.

If you want to order your men to attack
the dreygur with swords, go to 48.
To shoot the dreygur with arrows, go to 27.

22

"Stand and fight!" you order your men. "Use your shields to block the venom!"

Your men attack with swords and spears, keeping the cats at bay. But their weapons cannot harm the beasts, and you know this is a battle you cannot win. You look around for a way to escape.

If you want to order your men to climb trees to escape the cats, go to 36.

If you would rather order them to swim across the river, go to 49.

23

"Loki!" you cry. "Save us!"

A crack opens in the mountainside and Loki appears. "Fenrir!" he cries. "Son!"

The terrible wolf slinks to Loki's side like a whipped dog.

Loki turns to you. "The mighty deeds your warriors have done in my name deserve my aid."

The air is full of snow. Loki and Fenrir disappear into the blizzard.

You rally your remaining men. "Warriors, we must continue our quest. Let us ride on with brave hearts!"

After a hard journey, you cross into the northlands of your country.

Go to 14.

24

You remember just in time your harpist's tale of a warrior defeating an undead foe by cutting off its head.

You swing your blade at the blood-bride's neck. Her face freezes in horror. Then, as her headless body slumps to the earth, you cry out to your men. "Use your swords and do as I do."

Your surviving men follow your example and make short work of destroying the remaining blood-brides.

Agnar leans on his sword. "We should burn our dead comrades and the men of the village," he says.

If you agree, go to 3.
If you insist on pressing on, go to 38.

25

You lower your sword. "Soldiers of this castle!" you cry. "I am Beowulf, King of the Geats, and your lord. Break this enchanter's foul spell and remember where your true loyalty lies!"

The ghosts hesitate. Then they drop their weapons, and bow to you.

You look for Magnus, but the enchanter has disappeared.

You hear a footstep behind you. A small girl is walking hesitantly towards you. "Sir," she says, "have you beaten the enchanter? He has been holding me prisoner ..." She bursts into tears.

If you wish to help the girl, go to 33.
If you decide to question her, go to 13.

26

As you head towards Magnus's castle, the path you are on starts to rise, leading to a ruined graveyard — an eerie and dangerous-looking place. Rank grasses and stunted, leafless trees grow between its crumbling headstones and mouldering tombs. You feel a chill of terror as you look at it.

There is another path to your right. This leads into the marshy ground surrounding the graveyard on all sides; a bleak watery landscape covered in mist — the Dark Fens.

If you decide to head into the graveyard, go to 4.

If you think you should take the right-hand path, go to 11.

27

"Shoot them!" you cry.

Your men loose arrow after arrow at the dreygur. But though every one finds its mark, the dreygur are undead creatures and your shafts have no effect on them. Some have a dozen arrows sticking through them, and are still attacking.

Go to 39.

28

A crumbling bridge leads over a ravine to a great stone gateway. The wooden door to the main castle courtyard stands half open on rusted iron hinges.

You walk around the castle walls. They are high, but the stone looks uneven and there are gaps in the battlements. The climb would not be too hard.

On the far side of the castle you find another, much smaller door, with steps going down. You decide that these must lead to an underground crypt.

If you decide to go through the main door, go to 37.

If you would rather climb the walls, go to 17.

If you would prefer to go down into the crypt, go to 10.

29

"Thor!" you cry. "Save us!"

The thunder god appears. He flies at the Midgard Serpent, hammer ready to strike. The terrible creature releases your ship and sinks below the waves.

Thor turns to you. "Your warriors have honoured me by their mighty deeds. Such courage deserves my aid."

Mist rises from the sea and the god disappears. You call on your remaining men to repair the ship and get under way.

After a long, hard voyage, you arrive at a harbour in the northlands. Leaving the ship, you head for the nearest village.

Go to 14.

30

You order your men to press on. After a short march you arrive at another village. This one seems undamaged and there are no signs of fire or attack — but it seems to be deserted.

If you decide to send your men to search the village, go to 15.

If you would rather keep your men together, go to 8.

31

"Leave them!" you order.

Some of your men grumble at your hard-heartedness. Torvald, defying your command, strokes a kitten's head.

The moment he touches it, the tiny creature

grows into a monstrous cat with glowing red eyes. It spits at Torvald, who puts his hands to his face, screaming in agony. Then he falls to the ground, dead.

Your men draw their swords and pull back. "A palug cat!" you cry. "More devilry of Magnus!

The harpist says they spit deadly venom!"

The rest of the kittens transform. You look around for ways to escape.

If you want to order your men to climb trees to escape the cats, go to 36.

If you would rather order them to swim across the river, go to 49.

32

"Keep going!" you tell your men. "This marsh is not endless."

You see a light — a lantern, guiding you to safety! Then you step into even deeper mud, and the light disappears. You realise that it was another will-o'-the-wisp and as you try to pull your legs out of the clinging mud, you discover that you are stuck. In vain you cry for help, thrash frantically at the shallow water, grasp desperately at the clumps of coarse grass. Stagnant water fills your mouth. Then foul-tasting mud clogs your throat and nostrils, as you are drawn deep into the mire to drown.

You've been swamped! Not a heroic way to go. Go back to 1.

33

You drop your sword and take the girl's hand. "Don't be afraid," you tell her, "everything will be all right ..."

You feel the child's hand suddenly grow in yours as she transforms into Magnus. You had forgotten that the enchanter was a shape-changer!

Smiling savagely, Magnus points his staff at your heart. A blast of light bursts from it and you feel your life force ebb away.

You forgot to be careful, and have paid the price! Go to 1.

34

Your warriors arm themselves and put on warm cloaks. It is midwinter and the journey will be long and cold.

Your battle-chief, Agnar, comes to report. "The men are ready. Shall we head north by land, or by sea?"

You consider. A long ride through the snow will be hard on the men and their horses. Travelling by sea, you risk storms and the threat of ice, but may save time.

If you decide to travel by land, go to 45.

If you decide to travel by sea, go to 7.

35

"What plague has made your men sick and left you unharmed?" you ask. "Are you truly the women of this village?"

You reach out and grab the hand of one of the women. "Your hand is clean and unmarked by toil," you tell her. "Women of the northlands have to work hard to survive. Who are you?"

The leader of the women tries to soothe you. "All your questions will be answered," she says. "But first you must rest."

If you want to rest, go to 19.

If you wish to draw your sword, go to 46.

36

You and your men break away from the cats, and climb into the trees surrounding the farmhouse. Reaching a safe height, you breathe a sigh of relief.

Then you hear a scratching sound from below and the tree begins to shake. Too late, you remember that cats are great climbers! You look down into burning red eyes, and feel a terrible pain as claws dig into your leg.

You are dragged from your perch. As you lie
in the snow, a palug cat pounces. Its savage
jaws tear into your flesh. You try to fight off the
fearsome creature, but it is too powerful.

Pain wracks your body, and you die with the
sounds of screaming in your ears.

**Are you a mouse? Whatever you are,
you're no legend! Go to 1.**

37

If Magnus is powerful enough to put so many
obstacles in your path, he will be prepared for a
sneak attack.

You cross the bridge to the crumbling gateway.
You force the door fully open, and go through
the castle until you find yourself in the ruined
Great Hall. Human bones, armour and weapons
litter the floor.

On a raised platform at the end of the hall
stands a tall, cloaked figure holding a glowing
staff. "I am Magnus," it says. "You will never
defeat me!"

The wizard raises his staff. Ghosts of long-
dead soldiers flow from the walls, and rise up

through the floor. They collect weapons and armour as they race to attack you.

If you want to fight the ghosts, go to 5.

If you want to order them to lay down their weapons, go to 25.

38

"We must press on," you say. "Who knows what evils Magnus may commit while we delay?"

You leave the village behind. After an hour, you arrive at a lonely farmhouse surrounded by trees, with a river running alongside. Slaughtered cattle, sheep and goats surround the farm. The air is full of the stink of death.

One of your men, Torvald, opens the door of a barn. Out creeps a litter of kittens, crying piteously.

"At least these poor creatures have survived," says Torvald, reaching down to stroke one.

If you agree your men can rescue the kittens, go to 16.

If you decide to order your men to leave the kittens, go to 31.

39

You remember your harpist singing of a hero who overcame a dreygur by wrestling it back into its grave and holding it there until dawn. You can think of no other way to beat the monster.

You disarm the dreygur and grapple with it.

Your fingers clutch rotting flesh, and the terrible smell of decay tears at your nostrils. Moaning and gibbering, the creature fights back, but you are too strong for it. You force it into its grave and hold it there until the first rays of the sun creep across the graveyard. As they touch the dreygur, it sinks back into the earth.

You look around. All the dreygur are gone. But so are your men. You are the lone survivor of the quest.

You look up at the sinister ruins of Magnus's castle.

Go to 28.

40

"Loki!" you cry. "Save us!"

Loki rises from the waves: but he only shakes his head at your plight. "The serpent will not obey me," he says. "It will only listen to Thor, who once stunned it with his mighty hammer." A wave breaks against the ship and Loki disappears into the spray.

You open your mouth to summon Thor, but you are too late. The Midgard Serpent crushes your ship. The screams of your men fill your ears as you fall helplessly into the sea to drown.

**You've been sent for an early bath!
Go to 1.**

41

In vain, you try to raise your sword to fight the evil enchanter.

Magnus laughs. "You are in my power. Your hands will not move. You can do me no harm."

You struggle, but cannot break free of the enchanter's spell. Magnus points his staff at you. There is a brilliant white flash, then the darkness of death.

Heroes of legend make better choices. If you wish to prove yourself worthy, go to 1.

42

You turn the polished blade of your sword until it shows you the girl's reflection. This is no lost, helpless child; it is Magnus the Enchanter.

Magnus drops the illusion and transforms into his true shape. The wizard raises his staff to blast you into eternity. But he is too slow. You whirl round and throw your sword overarm. It spins through the air and buries itself to the hilt in Magnus's chest.

The enchanter's body collapses to the floor, but his ghost remains upright, staring at you in horror. The ghosts of the castle close in and drag it away.

Go to 50.

43

You point at the hoard. "Take what you want!
The dead have no need of wealth."

Most of your men rush greedily towards
the pile of gold. As soon as they touch it, the
earth shudders and armed figures rise from
every grave. They are dreygur, the most feared
creatures of the undead realm — immensely
strong flesh-eating zombies of slain warriors.

Your men reach for weapons from the hoard,
but they are too late. The dreygur cut them
down. You have no time to defend yourself; your
end is brutal, but mercifully quick.

**You should not have allowed your men
to be overcome with greed! Go to 1.**

44

"Run!" you cry.

Your men take to their heels. But cats are
hunters, and will chase anything. All around you,
cats pounce on your comrades. The yowls of the
savage beasts and the shrieks of dying men echo
in your ears.

You feel a sudden great weight on your back.

You fall, and the cat's terrible jaws meet around your neck, before darkness descends.

Look what the cat's dragged in! You are no legend. Go back to 1.

45

"Saddle the horses," you tell Agnar. "We go by land."

You trek into the mountains, your horses battling their way through drifts and skidding on icy paths.

A terrifying snarl sets your horse rearing and whinnying in fear. Blocking the mountain pass in front of you is a gigantic wolf — it is Fenrir!

Your warriors attack, but arrows and spears bounce off the wolf's tough hide.

"This is a creature of the gods, and only they can fight it!" Agnar says. "Call upon the gods of our people — Thor or Loki — to help us!"

If you want to call upon Thor, go to 12.
If you want to call upon Loki, go to 23.

46

"To arms, men!" you order, drawing your sword. "These are creatures of Magnus!"

You watch in horror as the women reveal their true natures. They are blood-brides — evil, undead creatures that survive by drinking human blood!

Some of your men are too slow. They scream as the women attack them with fingernails turned into razor-sharp claws, and teeth as deadly as knives.

The woman whose hand you examined stalks you, wary of your sword. You rack your brains to remember how to deal with these terrible creatures.

If you want to stab at the body of the blood-bride, go to 6.
If you decide to cut off her head, go to 24.

"You lie! You are not Magnus's prisoner!" you cry. "You are Magnus the enchanter in the shape of a girl!"

The girl wrings her hands and pleads, "No! Please help me!"

You hesitate. At that moment, the girl transforms into the enchanter, who points his staff at you.

You try to raise your sword, but you are too late! A terrible, evil light bursts from the enchanter's staff and surrounds you. Your life is ripped from your body, and whirls away into eternal darkness.

He who hesitates is lost! Go to 1.

The nearest dreygur attacks you. You thrust hard, running your blade through its body. Your opponent seems not even to notice the blow. You realise that the undead creature can feel no pain, and no fear.

You attack again, cutting the dreygur's head off with a great sweep of your sword. The creature merely picks its head up and puts it back on.

You realise that you must find another way to defeat the dreygur.

Go to 39.

49

"The river!" you cry. "Swim for your lives!"

You run and dive into the river, and your remaining men follow quickly behind you. The palug cats set up a disappointed yowling as the icy water carries you and your comrades swiftly away.

Within a short while, you hear the sound of roaring water ahead. The speed of the current becomes faster. You are being carried towards a waterfall! You must reach the riverbank before you are swept to your doom.

If you want to take off your armour and drop your weapons to help you swim, go to 9.

If you would rather keep your armour and weapons, go to 20.

Your people gather as you return to your Feast Hall. There is joy at your safe return, but weeping for your companions who will never come home again.

Osric, the blind harpist, greets you. "Lord Beowulf, once more you have rid our land of a terrible curse. You are a hero. This great deed of yours will pass into legend!"

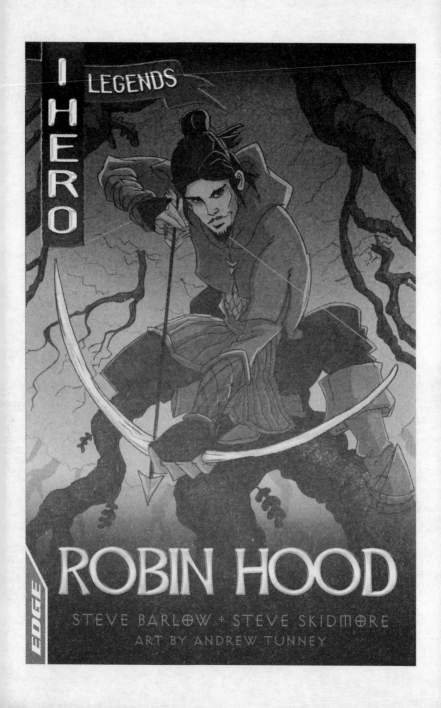

I HERO

LEGENDS

ROBIN HOOD

STEVE BARLOW + STEVE SKIDMORE
ART BY ANDREW TUNNEY

EDGE

You are Robin Hood. You live in Sherwood Forest with your band of outlaws including Little John, Friar Tuck, Will Scarlett and Maid Marian.

King Richard the Lionheart rules England, but has been captured in the East. His brother, John, rules England in his place, helped by his evil supporters including the Sheriff of Nottingham and his deputy, Guy of Gisborne.

Your band of outlaws are sworn to fight injustice and defend the rights of ordinary people. To do this, you rob from the rich to give to the poor.

You have had information that a merchant is going to be passing through Sherwood Forest. He has a box of gold coins, collected by overcharging his customers and crooked dealing. You head into the heart of the forest ...

Continue the adventure in:

iHERO LEGENDS
ROBIN HOOD

About the 2Steves

"The 2Steves" are
Britain's most popular
writing double act
for young people,
specialising in comedy
and adventure. They
perform regularly in schools and libraries,
and at festivals, taking the power of words
and story to audiences of all ages.

Together they have written many books,
including the *I HERO Immortals* and *iHorror* series.

About the illustrator:
Andrew Tunney (aka 2hands)

Andrew is a freelance artist and writer based in
Manchester, UK. He has worked in illustration, character
design, comics, print, clothing and live-art. His work
has been featured by Comics Alliance, ArtSlant Street,
DigitMag, The Bluecoat, Starburst and Forbidden Planet.
He earned the nickname "2hands" because he can draw
with both hands at once. He is not ambidextrous; he just
works hard.

Have you completed the I HERO Quests?

Battle to save an underwater world in Atlantis Quest:

978 1 4451 2867 2 pb
978 1 4451 2867 9 ebook

978 1 4451 2870 2 pb
978 1 4451 2871 9 ebook

978 1 4451 2876 4 pb
978 1 4451 2877 1 ebook

978 1 4451 2873 3 pb
978 1 4451 2874 0 ebook

Defeat the Red Queen in Blood Crown Quest:

978 1 4451 1499 6 pb
978 1 4451 1503 0 ebook

978 1 4451 1500 9 pb
978 1 4451 1504 7 ebook

978 1 4451 1501 6 pb
978 1 4451 1505 4 ebook

978 1 4451 1502 3 pb
978 1 4451 1506 1 ebook

Also by the 2Steves...

978 1 4451 4081 0 pb
978 1 4451 4082 7 eBook

Immortals

HERO

Dragon

Steve Barlow – Steve Skidmore

You are the last Dragon Warrior.
A dark, evil force stirs within the
Iron Mines. Grull the Cruel's
army is on the march! YOU must
stop Grull.

978 1 4451 4088 9 pb
978 1 4451 4087 2 eBook

Immortals

HERO

Mermaid

Steve Barlow – Steve Skidmore

You are a noble mermaid –
your father is King Edmar.
The Tritons are attacking your home
of Coral City. YOU must save the Merrow
people by finding the Lady of the Sea.

978 1 4451 4084 1 pb
978 1 4451 4085 8 eBook

Immortals

HERO

Superhero

Steve Barlow – Steve Skidmore

You are Olympian, a superhero.
Your enemy, Doctor Robotic,
is turning people into mind slaves.
Now YOU must put a stop to his
plans before it's too late!

978 1 4451 3958 6 pb
978 1 4451 3961 6 eBook

Immortals

HERO

Wizard

Steve Barlow – Steve Skidmore

You are a young wizard.
The evil Witch Queen has captured
Prince Bron. Now YOU must rescue
him before she takes control of
Nine Mountain kingdom!